"I want to hire you," said the boy. "My name is Algernon Kehoe. Some big kid just made off with Minnie and Moocher."

"Kidnapped them?" exclaimed Encyclopedia. "Didn't they shout for help?"

"No, but they clinked a little," said Algernon glumly.

Encyclopedia couldn't imagine why two girls should dress in anything that clinked, like two knights or a pair of dice.

The case was a puzzler, all right.

"Describe the missing persons, please," he said.

"Minnie has two red stripes across the middle," began Algernon. "Moocher has—wait! They're not missing persons. They're missing marbles."

**ENCYCLOPEDIA BROWN
Gets His Man**

HEY, KIDS!

Do you have a wacky story to tell about an animal, a fact, a crime, a sport? The funnier and wackier the better! But it must be *true*.

You can write about it, or enclose a clipping from your local newspaper, or send a note from your parents or teacher verifying the story. If it is included in an Encyclopedia Brown book, your name will appear in the book.

Send your wacky true story (along with your name and address) to: Encyclopedia Brown, c/o Bantam Books, 666 Fifth Avenue, New York 10103.

ENCYCLOPEDIA BROWN
Gets His Man
By DONALD J. SOBOL

Illustrated by
Leonard Shortall

A BANTAM SKYLARK BOOK

*This low-priced Bantam Book
has been completely reset in a type face
designed for easy reading, and was printed
from new plates. It contains the complete
text of the original hard-cover edition.*
NOT ONE WORD HAS BEEN OMITTED.

RL 6, IL 5-up

ENCYCLOPEDIA BROWN GETS HIS MAN

*A Bantam Skylark Book / published by arrangement with
Thomas Nelson, Inc., Publishers*

PRINTING HISTORY

*Thomas Nelson edition published September 1967
7 printings through 1978*

Bantam Skylark edition / September 1978

2nd printing . . . . . . *October 1978*	*5th printing* . . . . *November 1979*
3rd printing . . . . *May 1979*	*6th printing* . . . . *March 1980*
4th printing . . . . *July 1979*	*7th printing* . . . . *May 1980*

All rights reserved.
Copyright © 1967 by Donald J. Sobol.
*This book may not be reproduced in whole or in part, by
mimeograph or any other means, without permission.
For information address: Elsevier/Nelson Books,
Division of Elsevier-Dutton Publishing Co., Inc.
2 Park Ave., New York, N.Y. 10016.*

ISBN 0-553-15136-3

Published simultaneously in the United States and Canada

---

*Bantam Books are published by Bantam Books, Inc. Its trademark, consisting of the
words "Bantam Books" and the portrayal of a bantam, is Registered in U.S. Patent
and Trademark Office and in other countries. Marca Registrada. Bantam Books, Inc.,
666 Fifth Avenue, New York, New York 10103.*

PRINTED IN THE UNITED STATES OF AMERICA

18 17 16 15 14 13 12 11 10 9

For
My Son
Glenn

Contents

ENCYCLOPEDIA BROWN
Gets His Man

The Case of
the Marble Shooter

Now it happens that in America some people break the law.

Many get caught, but a few get away.

This was not true in Idaville.

In Idaville *everyone* who broke the law got caught.

Aside from catching crooks one—two—three, Idaville was like any other American town its size. It had banks, movie theaters, and delicatessens. It had rich families, poor families, and several miles of sunny beach.

And for its war on crime, Idaville had Encyclopedia Brown.

Encyclopedia's father was Chief Brown, head of the Idaville police force. People from everywhere agreed that he was the smartest police officer in the land.

Chief Brown never let out the reason for his success. If he did, who would believe him?

Who would believe that the real brains behind Idaville's wonderful police record was his quiet, ten-year-old son?

For a year now Chief Brown had been bringing home his hardest cases. Encyclopedia solved them while eating dinner in the Brown's red brick house on Rover Avenue.

Since Encyclopedia had taken to matching wits with criminals, the word had raced through the underworld: *"Stay clear of Idaville."*

Idaville! Big-time gunmen trembled at the mere mention of the town!

Encyclopedia never told anyone about the help he gave his father. He didn't want to seem different from other fifth-graders.

But he could do nothing about his nickname.

Only his parents and teachers called him by his right name, Leroy. Everyone else in Idaville called him Encyclopedia.

An encyclopedia is a book or set of books

filled with facts from A to Z. Encyclopedia Brown knew about the American Automobile Association, the Zanzibar Zipper Company, and everything in between. He had read more books than Miss Babcock, the principal of the Idaville grammar school.

Encyclopedia did not solve mysteries just in the dining room. During the summer he often solved them in the garage.

He wanted to help the children of the neighborhood. So he had opened his own detective business.

Outside the garage each morning he hung a sign:

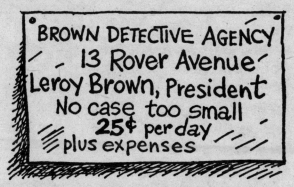

One day a boy walked into the garage. He dropped to one knee before Idaville's only private detective.

"Goodness," thought Encyclopedia. "I haven't been *that* successful!"

The boy wasn't doing homage, however. He was aiming. With a snap of his thumb he spun a quarter through the air. It landed on the gasoline can beside Encyclopedia.

"You've got a hot thumb," said Encyclopedia. "You've got the hottest thumb I've ever seen."

"I want to hire you," said the boy. "My name is Algernon Kehoe. Some big kid just made off with Minnie and Moocher."

"Kidnapped them?" exclaimed Encyclopedia. "Didn't they shout for help?"

"No, but they clinked a little," said Algernon glumly.

Encyclopedia couldn't imagine why two girls should dress in anything that clinked, like two knights or a pair of dice.

"It's months too early for Halloween," he thought.

The case was a puzzler, all right.

"Describe the missing persons, please," he said.

"Minnie has two red stripes across the middle," began Algernon. "Moocher has—wait! They're not missing persons. They're missing marbles."

Algernon explained. Minnie and Moocher were his best shooters. He had been practicing marbles by himself when a big kid had come along and challenged him to a match.

"For fair or for keeps?" asked Encyclopedia.

"For keeps," answered Algernon.

"He beat you?"

"I beat him," said Algernon. "I won all his marbles. He got sore and took Minnie and Moocher, and all my other marbles."

"You didn't try to stop him?"

"Of course I tried," said Algernon. "I said I'd tweek him, but a bunch of his friends appeared. They asked who I was, and the big kid said, 'Who? I don't see anyone.' But I noticed he closed his eyes just before he spoke."

"Hmmm," said Encyclopedia. "How was he dressed?"

"He wore a sweatshirt with 'Tigers' written on it, like his friends."

"I knew it!" exclaimed Encyclopedia. "Bugs Meany!"

Bugs Meany was the leader of the Tigers, a gang of tough older boys. When it came to upsetting the peace of the neighborhood, they were worse than noisy plumbing. Since opening his detective agency, Encyclopedia had often been hired to stop Bugs's dishonest doings.

For several minutes Encyclopedia was silent, thinking.

Algernon stood by, working his thumb to develop muscle.

Finally Encyclopedia said, "Bugs will say he never saw you before. We must make him admit he knows you."

"He knows me," said Algernon. "He called me 'Algernon' and 'old pal' when we started to shoot marbles. After I licked him, he called me a 'dirty thief' and lots of other names."

"We had better talk with Bugs," said Encyclopedia. "Let's go, Algernon."

"Just call me Al, if you don't mind. Algernon means 'with the mustache.' "

The Tiger's clubhouse was an unused tool shed behind Mr. Sweeny's Auto Body Shop. When Encyclopedia and Algernon arrived, Bugs was alone. He was playing checkers with himself, and cheating.

"Scram," he snarled when he saw Encyclopedia. "Or I'll knock you so hard on the head you'll have to take off your shoes to watch television."

"I ought to tweek him now while he's alone," whispered Al.

"Take it easy," Encyclopedia whispered back.

But Algernon began working his thumb excitedly.

Bugs Meany stared. "What's with this kid?" he asked. "Is he practicing to be a hitch-hiker?"

"His name is Al Kehoe, and you stole Minnie and Moocher and his other marbles," said Encyclopedia. "Kindly return them."

"*I* stole his marbles?" cried Bugs. He clapped himself smartly on the forehead. "Why, I never saw Jumpy Thumb here before in my life."

Algernon's marble-shooting thumb was wiggling faster than ever. "I was a coward to let him rob me," he muttered. He started for Bugs.

Encyclopedia pushed him back.

"I'm going to tweek him, so help me," said Algernon.

Just then Duke Kelly and Spike Larsen,

"I stole his marbles?" cried Bugs.

two Tigers, entered the clubhouse. They glared at Encyclopedia. Then they saw Algernon's thumb wiggling.

"Who is *he*?" they asked.

"Algernon Kehoe," answered Bugs. "He says I stole his marbles."

"I ought to tweek them all," Algernon growled under his breath. "Tweek, tweek, tweek."

"What's he mumbling about?" demanded Bugs.

"I beat you at marbles, and I can beat you at tweek," said Algernon.

"Tweek?" said Bugs.

"Tweek," repeated Algernon. "It's played like this."

His right hand, with his powerful thumb tucked under his forefinger, shot out. When his hand got under Bugs's lower lip, his thumb snapped free like a broken spring.

"Tweek!" said Algernon.

Boing! Boing! went Bugs's lips. They bounced up and down like the tip of a diving board.

While Bugs danced around, flapping his arms in pain, Spike and Duke cocked their fists.

Encyclopedia held up his hands.

"Don't make more trouble for your-selves," he warned. "Bugs stole Algernon's marbles all right."

WHAT MADE ENCYCLOPEDIA SO SURE?

(Turn to page 103 for the solution to The Case of the Marble Shooter.)

The Case of
Bugs Meany, Detective

Whenever Encyclopedia crossed his path, Bugs Meany burned with a single desire.

It was to fill Encyclopedia's mouth with a fist.

But Bugs never swung a blow. Every time he felt like it, his jaw ached. For he remembered the detective's junior partner, Sally Kimball.

Sally was the prettiest girl in the fifth grade. She was also the best athlete.

The first time she had seen Bugs, he was bullying a Cub Scout.

Sally had jumped off her bike. She had put her left into Bugs's face *rap-tap-tap*. Then her right had gone *whammo!*

15

After the first punch, Bugs had seen red. After ten punches, he had seen stars.

"Bugs is like a lumpy mattress," warned Encyclopedia. "He won't rest till he gets even."

"He's just a big bully," said Sally. "He can't match your fast brainwork."

But the next morning Sally was worried.

"Look what was under my front door!" She handed Encyclopedia a business card. It read:

Tigers, Inc.
Private Detectives
Staff of Experts
20¢ A Day Plus Expenses
Office Behind Sweeny's Body Shop

"Bugs is out to steal your customers," said Sally angrily. "He's charging a nickel less."

"Bugs can't charge anything till he gets a case," replied Encyclopedia.

"He *has* a case," said Sally. "Mario Martinelli hired him to find his violin."

Encyclopedia gasped. "Golly, Mario has been practicing hard for the summer symphony orchestra. Tryouts are tomorrow!"

"Bugs will never find the violin in time. His *experts* couldn't find a clam in a sand pail," said Sally. "If we don't help Mario, he won't make the orchestra. Come on!"

Encyclopedia agreed reluctantly. He reached for his bike. "Bugs has every right to complain if we butt in," he said.

As the partners neared Mario's house, they could not believe their eyes.

Tigers were crawling over the lawn, peering through magnifying glasses for clues. Bugs was dusting fingerprint powder on a windowsill.

Mario, a slender boy of eleven, watched uneasily.

"No fingerprints here," called Bugs. "The thief wiped the windowsill clean. We're up against a master criminal!"

"Won't you be able to find my violin?" asked Mario.

"Don't worry, maestro. I'm a regular bloodhound," said Bugs. "I'm onto something right now." He grinned mysteriously.

The grin vanished as he spied Encyclopedia and Sally. "Hey, you Tigers," he shouted. "Let's go. This place is getting crowded with amateurs."

After the Tigers had trooped off, Encyclopedia asked Mario about the theft.

"Someone climbed through my open bedroom window last night and stole the violin," answered Mario.

"Why did you hire Bugs Meany?" asked Sally.

"He came by early this morning. He was passing out his business cards," said Mario. "I told him about the violin. I said my mother had already telephoned the police. Bugs insisted he was smarter than any policeman."

"All those Tigers working for twenty cents," mused Sally. "Something is fishy!"

"Oh, there is a ten-dollar reward," said Mario. "Bugs told my mother we would have a better chance of getting the violin back if she offered a reward."

"That no-good Bugs!" cried Sally. "I'll bet anything he stole the violin himself!"

"If he did, I'll surely get it back," said Mario hopefully.

The three children sat down on the porch. There was nothing to do but wait for Bugs to return with the "stolen" violin and claim the reward.

An hour later the Tigers paraded back.

Sure enough, Bugs was carrying the violin.

"Man, oh, man!" he sang. "I guess you know now who is the greatest detective in Idaville!"

The rest of the Tigers threw up their arms and cheered like mad. "Bugs! Bugs! Bugs!"

"While certain private detectives were sitting around helpless, I was using my head," said Bugs. "To find stolen goods, you have to think like a thief."

"You've had enough practice," snapped Sally.

Before Bugs could take a fighting stance, Encyclopedia spoke up. "How did you find the violin, Bugs?"

"I'll show you," said Bugs, relieved at not having to defend himself against Sally.

They all walked to the woods past Rolling Road.

"I figured some kid had swiped the violin, hoping to collect a reward for its safe return," said Bugs. "A grownup thief would have stolen the silverware instead."

"That makes sense," said Mario.

"The thief couldn't take the stolen violin home," went on Bugs. "And if he wanted a reward, he had to hide it where it

The Tigers cheered like mad.

wouldn't get damaged. A tree seemed a good place—that's exactly where I saw it. Up in the top of that one."

Encyclopedia looked at the tree to which Bugs had pointed. "But you can't see to the top," he said. "The leaves are too thick."

"Y-you can't? W-well—why—a squirrel helped me," stammered Bugs. "Yeah, this squirrel was on the trunk, halfway between the ground and the lowest branch. Something made it nervous. It backed down slowly, reached the ground, and raced away."

"Then you climbed the tree to see why the squirrel acted so strangely," said Encyclopedia. "And lo! There was the violin!"

"Right! You'll be a detective yet," said Bugs. "Now pardon me while I go and collect the reward."

"There is no reward for liars," retorted Encyclopedia.

WHY DIDN'T ENCYCLOPEDIA BELIEVE BUGS?

(Turn to page 104 for the solution to The Case of Bugs Meany, Detective.)

The Case of
the Underwater Car

When Encyclopedia and his pals went camping overnight in the State Park, they had a rule: Never take Benny Breslin along.

Everyone liked Benny—during the day.

At night Benny became a public enemy by climbing into bed. He closed his eyes, opened his mouth, and sounded his nose. His snoring shook garage doors up and down the street.

"You should take Benny with you this trip," said Encyclopedia's mother.

"The last time we took Benny camping," replied Encyclopedia, "the governor closed the State Park for two days."

It was true. Benny's snores had

awakened other campers. Frightened, they had reported a wild animal in the area. The park had been closed for two days while state troopers hunted a bear.

"Benny's mother bought him a strap," said Mrs. Brown. "It fits under his nose. He sleeps very quietly now."

"Quietly," thought Encyclopedia, "as an elephant choking to death."

Nevertheless, he agreed to take Benny. He could not say no after his mother gave him a box of cotton.

"You can stuff your ears," said Mrs. Brown. "There's enough for everyone."

After lunch Encyclopedia biked down to Mill Creek. Benny Breslin was already there, and so were the other boys of the gang: Charlie Stewart, Fangs Liveright, Pinky Plummer, Herb Stein, and Billy and Jody Turner.

They reached the State Park two hours later. Most of the best camping sites were taken. The only good spot left was on a small hill overlooking a bend in the dirt road. Beyond the road, and about forty feet below it, was the ocean.

The boys unpacked their bicycles,

pitched their tents, and went down to the ocean with their fishing poles.

By nightfall, no one except Benny had hooked any fish big enough to keep. Benny had caught seven beauties.

"Fish are great music lovers," explained Benny. "Just sing them a scale. A-ha-ha-ha!"

He had caught three fish humming *The Muffin Man* and four with *Rock-a-Bye-Baby*. However, Encyclopedia noticed Benny was the only boy using shrimp, not worms, for bait.

"It has to be the bait," thought Encyclopedia. "Benny's singing is even worse than his snoring."

Charlie Stewart got a fire blazing, and Pinky Plummer fried the fish. After eating, the boys sat around the fire talking baseball for three hours. Then they turned in.

Encyclopedia had Benny for a tentmate. Benny lay down in his bedroll, barefaced.

"Haven't you forgotten something?" asked Encyclopedia, horrified.

"My strap!" cried Benny, feeling his nose. "I left my strap at home!"

"Well, it doesn't matter," said Encyclo-

The boys went down to the ocean.

pedia bravely. He did not want to hurt Benny's feelings by passing out the cotton before Benny was asleep.

In no time at all, Benny began to snore for all he was worth.

Encyclopedia opened the box of cotton and gave some to each boy. They plugged their ears. It didn't help.

"Looks like a long night," moaned Charlie Stewart. "Benny's giving it both nostrils."

Encyclopedia lay down with his ear next to Benny's ear. He reasoned that he was thus as far from the terrible snorts, sneezes, and rasps as Benny himself, and Benny was gloriously asleep.

Reason, however, was no match for Benny's nose. After half a minute, Encyclopedia squirmed to the far side of the tent and groaned quietly.

One by one the boys fell asleep from sheer weariness. By two o'clock in the morning, Encyclopedia's ears felt black and blue. He pocketed his flashlight and went out for a walk in the cool night air.

As he reached the dirt road, a car suddenly appeared. It moved slowly. Encyclopedia stopped and observed the car from behind a tree. The road curved, but the car continued straight on.

The driver jumped out as the car crashed through the railing. He watched the car roll toward the ocean. Then he smoothed a place in the dirt and lay down.

"Help!" he hollered. "Help! My back! Somebody help me!"

Several campers rushed from the woods and crowded around him. Encyclopedia walked to the point where the car had gone off the road and flashed his light down the rocky slope.

The car had stopped halfway down between the road and the ocean. It rested on its top, a complete wreck. About the only things undamaged were the four worn-out tires. They still spun in the air.

All at once the rocks beneath the car gave way. The car slid into the water and disappeared below the surface.

"The driver's name is Matthew Starr," said Chief Brown at dinner that evening. "He claims he fell asleep at the wheel and woke up just in time to escape going off the road with the car."

"I told you what really happened!" protested Encyclopedia.

"You were the only witness," said Chief Brown. Mr. Starr's lawyer will say it was dark and that you were not fully awake."

"Somebody ought to shove his lawyer into a pup tent with Benny Breslin," muttered Encyclopedia.

"The car was brand new and cost six thousand dollars," said Chief Brown. "Mr. Starr wants the insurance company to pay him for it. But more important, he says he hurt his back in the accident and can't work any more."

"A doctor can prove he's faking the injury," said Encyclopedia.

"I'm afraid not," said Chief Brown. "Bad backs are a kind of injury that can't be disproved. Mr. Starr has a big policy with the insurance company. It will pay him money each month for the rest of his life if he can't work."

"The insurance company wants you to prove he wrecked his car on purpose. Then the insurance company won't have to pay him anything. Is that right?" asked Encyclopedia.

"Yes," replied Chief Brown. "But we can't get heavy machinery onto the dirt road to pull the car out of the ocean. Even if we could, I don't know what we would find to prove Mr. Starr wrecked his car on purpose."

"I know," said Encyclopedia.

WHAT HAD ENCYCLOPEDIA SEEN?

(Turn to page 105 for the solution to The Case of the Underwater Car.)

The Case of
the Whistling Ghost

Fabius Manning crawled slowly into the Brown Detective Agency.

Encyclopedia was in no way startled to see Fabius so close to the ground. During the summer, Fabius usually went about on his hands and knees.

Fabius studied bugs of all kinds. Nobody in Idaville knew more about the hidden desires of bee or beetle than Fabius.

Encyclopedia watched Fabius peering through a magnifying glass till the excitement grew unbearable.

"What is it?" Encyclopedia asked. "A *Coleoptera?*"

"Wrong," whispered Fabius, sneaking forward an inch.

"A *Dendroleon obsoletus?*"

"Wrong again," whispered Fabius. "A common stinkbug—ooops! You scared him off!"

"Sorry about that," said Encyclopedia.

Fabius arose sadly. But upon looking around and discovering where he was, he cheered up at once.

"Encyclopedia! Boy, I'm glad that bug led me here." He put twenty-five cents on the gasoline can. "I've been meaning to hire you."

"No case is too small," said Encyclopedia, hoping Fabius didn't take him at his word. Fabius might want a horsefly brought to justice. "What's the problem?"

"Somebody stole my camera," said Fabius. "I think the thief was a ghost."

Encyclopedia swallowed hard. "A g-ghost? *Where?*"

"In the old deserted Morgan house," said Fabius.

Encyclopedia recovered himself quickly. "I don't believe in ghosts. I believe in facts."

"The facts," announced Fabius. "Yesterday I went into the old house to hunt interesting bugs. I was about to photograph a spider when this ghost came down the stairway."

"You got the shakes and ran out of the house, leaving the camera behind?" said Encyclopedia.

"Right," said Fabius. "I raced out the front door so fast my own mother wouldn't have known me from a flying tank. An hour later, I went back for my camera. It was gone."

"Did you notice anything special about the ghost?"

"It was white as a sheet," said Fabius. "And it was making scary noises and whistling at the same time."

"It might have been a dog trainer in life," suggested Encyclopedia. "Let's go to the old Morgan house and look around."

Fabius got his bike, and the two boys rode to the "haunted" house. On the way they passed the home of Rocky Graham, one of Bugs Meany's Tigers.

Two blocks farther on was the old Morgan place. The big house had not been lived in for fifty years. It was a rotted wood building looking for a place to fall down.

The boys leaned their bikes against a pine tree. They walked through the hip-high grass and weeds, up onto the creaky front porch, and into the entrance hall.

"I left my camera at the foot of the stairs while I explored," said Fabius. "When I came back for it, there was the ghost, wailing and whistling."

He led the way into the kitchen.

"I wanted to photograph that!" he said, pointing to the back door.

Encyclopedia gasped in admiration. Across the lower half of the door a spider had spun a beautiful, wheel-shaped web.

"The best example I ever saw of the work of a *Theridiosoma radiosa*—otherwise called a ray spider," said Fabius in a glow.

While Fabius adored the spider web, Encyclopedia returned to the entrance hall. He found footprints in the heavy dust on the staircase.

"Ghosts don't wear shoes," he thought out loud. "At least not in the summer."

"How's that?" called Fabius. "Did you find a clue?"

"Your ghost left footprints," said Encyclopedia as Fabius hurried from the kitchen. "I think I know who it was."

"You're smarter than the FBI!" exclaimed Fabius. "Who was it?"

"The work of a ray spider," said Fabius.

"A boy who saw you come here with your camera yesterday," said Encyclopedia. "Rocky Graham."

"Aw, a lot of people could have seen me go into the house yesterday," said Fabius, disappointed. "Why Rocky Graham?"

"Because he lives close to this old house; because he's a member of the Tigers; and because he knocked out two front teeth a few days ago trying to break into a parked car."

"I heard that his screwdriver slipped and hit him in the mouth," said Fabius. "But what have two missing front teeth got to do with it?"

"Without his two front teeth," explained Encyclopedia, "whenever Rocky says the letter S, he *whistles*."

"The ape!" bellowed Fabius, hopping up and down in anger. "That rat in a bed-sheet!"

"Take it easy," said Encyclopedia. "We haven't any proof—yet. I want to hear what Rocky has to say for himself."

When the two boys arrived at the Graham house, Rocky was sitting on the ground groaning. He had just aimed a kick at a cat and missed, twisting his ankle.

"You dressed up in a sheet and scared me in the old Morgan house yesterday," said Fabius.

"Then you stole his camera," said Encyclopedia. "I'll bet a lot of people saw you go up the front porch. So don't deny it!"

Rocky's face showed how hard he was struggling for a fast alibi.

"Sure," he said, whistling a little. "Sure I saw you go inside. Another kid, carrying a sheet, went in just behind you. Pretty soon you came sailing out. I went inside to find out what was the matter. In the entrance hall I saw this other kid pick up a camera. When he spotted me, he ran out the back door and into the woods."

"That's a good story," said Encyclopedia. "Good enough to prove you were the thief!"

WHY?

(Turn to page 106 for the solution to The Case of the Whistling Ghost.)

The Case of
the Explorer's Money

"You haven't touched your breakfast, dear," said Mrs. Brown. "Is something wrong?"

"I'm not hungry," replied Chief Brown. "I'm worried."

"About a case?" asked Encyclopedia.

"Chief Walker of Glenn City wants me to help him recover fifty thousand dollars," said Chief Brown.

"Wow! Did someone rob a bank, Dad?"

"No, the money belongs to Sir Cameron Whitehead, who died last month. He was the famous Arctic explorer."

"Arctic—let's see," said Mrs. Brown. "That means just the North Pole region and not the South Pole area, doesn't it?"

"Yes, that's right," said Chief Brown. "Sir Cameron never went to the South Pole."

"But he made eleven trips to the North Pole," said Encyclopedia.

"Sir Cameron retired to Glenn City three years ago," said Chief Brown. "The money was stolen last month while he lay sick and dying. The Glenn City police still haven't found a clue."

Chief Brown drew a heavy breath. "Chief Walker of Glenn City thinks I can work a miracle. He expects me to capture the thief *presto!*"

"Why can't you?" asked Mrs. Brown. "You have a helper."

Chief Brown grinned. "Want to help, Leroy?"

"Go with you? Boy, would I!" exclaimed Encyclopedia. "I'll telephone Sally Kimball and tell her to look after the detective agency for the day."

Chief Brown went over the case during the half-hour drive to Glenn City.

The fifty thousand dollars had been stolen from a safe in the library of the explorer's home. The police believed the thief had hidden the money somewhere in or around the house, expecting to come back for it later.

The reason for this belief was simple. Anyone could get into Sir Cameron's house. But no one, including the servants, could leave the grounds without being searched by guards.

"Sir Cameron liked visitors," said Chief Brown. "However, he was afraid that someone might steal part of his famous Arctic collection. Ah, here's the estate just ahead."

Encyclopedia saw a large brick house and broad lawns enclosed by a high steel fence. A stream of people was entering by the main gate.

"Sir Cameron died the day after the theft," said Chief Brown. "All of his belongings—his house, his furniture, and his Arctic collection—are being auctioned today."

"Does Chief Walker think the thief will try to slip the money out in the crowd?" asked Encyclopedia.

"Yes, and there aren't enough policemen in the state to watch everyone here today."

As his father parked the car, a big man waved.

"That's Chief Walker. I'll be with him till the sale starts at ten o'clock," said Chief Brown. "Suppose we meet at the front door at ten minutes of ten."

Encyclopedia nodded and glanced at his watch. It was nine o'clock. That gave him fifty minutes to find the fifty thousand dollars!

The boy detective considered the thief's problem.

He could get into the house. But he could not get out of it without being searched by the guards. So after breaking open the safe, where would he hide the money?

Burying it in the ground would take too long. And someone was sure to see him. Then there was the risk of coming back later to dig up the money.

"The money has to be hidden where no one would think of looking," decided Encyclopedia.

He wandered from room to room. Men and women were examining every stick of furniture. Drawers were pulled out. Cabinet doors were opened. Wives argued with husbands about how much to bid for a chair or table or desk when the sale began.

Nobody screamed. Nobody fainted. Nobody opened a drawer or door and discovered fifty thousand dollars!

Encyclopedia edged up to a piano. Quickly he lifted the lid. Inside was only more piano. He searched on.

At nine-thirty he reached a long room. This was Sir Cameron's private museum. A sign above the door read:

Objects and Animals
From Sir Cameron Whitehead's
50 Years of Exploration
In the Lands of the Far North

In the center of the long room a life-like polar bear stood reared upon its hind legs. Eight little penguins formed a ring at the bear's feet.

More stuffed animals lined one wall. There were a wolverine, an Arctic fox, a caribou, a walrus, and other animals from the North Pole region.

The wall opposite the stuffed animals was hung with articles of Eskimo life: clothing, tools, weapons, and a sled made of driftwood with ivory-tipped runners.

The other two walls of the museum were

There were animals from the North Pole.

covered with photographs. Most of them showed Sir Cameron bundled up against snow and ice.

It was ten minutes before ten o'clock. Encyclopedia hurried to meet his father at the front door.

When Chief Brown arrived, he was frowning.

"I'm afraid it's hopeless," he said. "The Glenn City police have gone over every inch of the house and grounds. Somehow, the thief must have got past Sir Cameron's guards with the money."

"No, the money is still here, Dad," said Encyclopedia. "I think this is what happened. The thief waited till other visitors came to see the dying Sir Cameron. The thief went into the house with them bearing gifts.

"While the other visitors were in Sir Cameron's bedroom, the thief waited in the living room," went on Encyclopedia. "Once alone, he broke open the safe, stole the money, and hid it in the—"

IN THE WHAT?

(Turn to page 107 for the solution to The Case of the Explorer's Money.)

The Case of
the Coffee Smoker

Roscoe Kerr laid twenty-five cents on the gasoline can. His hand was trembling.

"I've got big problems," he said.

"Are you sure you want a detective, not a doctor?" said Encyclopedia. "You're shaking like a grass curtain."

Sally hurried over with an empty box. "Sit down before you drop," she said.

"I'll be all right," said Roscoe. "I've been smoking too many dried coffee grounds."

"You ought to change your brand," said Encyclopedia.

"I'd give up smoking, but it's too late," said Roscoe. "An hour ago I got a telephone call. The caller threatened to tell my mother I've been smoking—unless I paid him a dollar a week."

"That's blackmail!" gasped Encyclopedia.

"Who threatened you?" asked Sally.

"It sounded like Harry Hallahan," said Roscoe. "I wish I'd never seen him smoking behind the old library building!"

Harry Hallahan and the old library building had made news the month before. Harry had admitted to the police that he had been secretly smoking cigarettes behind the building. His carelessness had set it afire.

"He's been after me for reporting him," said Roscoe. "Whenever we meet, he strikes me."

"He walks up and socks you?" said Encyclopedia.

"No, he strikes me," said Roscoe, "on the seat with a wooden kitchen match and lights his pipe."

"You ought to wear your corduroy pants," said Encyclopedia.

"If I do," said Roscoe, "Harry makes me do a headstand. Then he strikes a match off the bottom of my shoe. He'll never forgive me for reporting him."

"It was your duty," said Sally.

"I know," said Roscoe. "But I forgot Harry is older than he looks. His seventeenth birthday was last week. His mother gave him permission to smoke a pipe with real tobacco anywhere he likes. He's been using me to light up ever since!"

"This is awful," said Sally. "Can't we do something, Encyclopedia?"

"Let's deal with the blackmail first," answered Encyclopedia. "Were you smoking today, Roscoe?"

"On and off all morning," said Roscoe. "I kept getting dizzy. I had to stop a lot for air."

"Puffing coffee in an old corncob pipe will do that to you," said Encyclopedia. "Where were you burning your lungs?"

"In the trees behind my house," said Roscoe.

Encyclopedia decided to examine the spot. On the way, Roscoe called himself every kind of a fool.

"Smoking always turns me green, but I thought I was being smart," he said. "If you get me out of this mess, Encyclopedia, I'll swear off smoking for life."

The three children went down the slope

behind Roscoe's house. Roscoe stopped in a group of trees.

"Usually I steal a smoke in my lean-to," he said. "Nobody can see me. But this morning I smoked under that oak tree."

Encyclopedia sat in Roscoe's lean-to. He could see nothing but the trees growing thickly in front. He moved to the oak. Now he could see one window of a neighboring house.

"The Hallahans live there," said Roscoe. "That window is Harry's room. But he isn't home."

"How do you know?" asked Sally.

"His parents went to Stuart Beach for the day," said Roscoe. "Mr. Hallahan is a fisherman. When he's away, Harry has to go out early in the morning to inspect the nets. He doesn't get back until about noon."

Encyclopedia's watch showed five minutes past noon. It also showed a raindrop.

The sky was clear except for a single black cloud. Suddenly the cloud seemed to open and the rain poured down.

Encyclopedia, Sally, and Roscoe darted

They darted into the lean-to.

into the lean-to. While they waited for the cloudburst to pass, Roscoe told about the telephone call.

"The blackmailer said to leave a dollar under the brown rock behind the statue of Thomas Edison tomorrow," he said.

"We can watch from hiding and catch him as he picks up the money!" said Sally.

"Harry will say he happened to kick aside the rock and saw the money by chance," said Encyclopedia. "No, we've got to talk with him before Roscoe pays a penny."

When the rain stopped, they climbed the hill to Harry's house. His father's truck was parked in front. The stone walk to the front door was under two inches of rainwater.

Roscoe scouted the rear. "The back walk is even wetter. There's no other way into the house," he said.

So the three children sloshed through the water to the front door. Sally rang the bell.

Harry shouted from the kitchen to come in. He was fixing himself lunch.

"You saw Roscoe smoking this morning from your bedroom window," said Encyclopedia. "Over the telephone you threatened to tell his mother unless he paid you a dollar a week."

"You're crazy as a jaybird!" said Harry. "I haven't been in my room since dawn. I've been on the water all morning."

"Don't tell us you just got home!" said Sally.

"I drove the truck back during the cloudburst," said Harry. "I waited in the truck till the rain stopped. Then I came straight into the kitchen."

Harry took his pipe from his pocket and filled it with tobacco. He reached into a box of kitchen matches on the stove.

"We know how you've been lighting your pipe!" said Sally.

Harry lifted a foot and struck a match on the bottom of his shoe. He was acting very superior.

"Stop blackmailing Roscoe," said Encyclopedia. "If you don't, he'll have to tell your father."

"Tell my father what?" sneered Harry.

"Tell him you stayed home all morning instead of inspecting the fishing nets," said Encyclopedia.

HOW DID ENCYCLOPEDIA KNOW?

(Turn to page 108 for the solution to The Case of the Coffee Smoker.)

The Case of
the Chinese Vase

When Encyclopedia tired of fighting crime, he often took a walk with Nevin Mercer.

Nevin was a gentle boy of twelve. He wanted to be a florist when he grew up.

The two boys enjoyed strolling about Idaville. They would stop to admire a rare tree or sniff a blossom.

Nevin's family was poor. To earn money, Nevin had gone into business cutting lawns. He used a power mower which Encyclopedia had helped him build from old parts.

Encyclopedia decided to find Nevin and take a nature walk. He had finished a case early. He had recovered Charlie Stewart's missing tooth collection.

"The collection wasn't stolen after all," Encyclopedia said to Sally. "Charlie's mother had used the teeth as weights in hanging out the wash. She put a few teeth in each of Charlie's stockings to keep them from getting tangled in the wind."

"Nice work," said Sally. "If his mother had left any teeth in the stockings, Charlie might have got his toenails clipped on the way to breakfast."

Encyclopedia sat down wearily. It was hard having a mother mixed up in a case.

"I'm taking the afternoon off," he said. "Maybe Nevin is free to visit the Botanical Gardens."

"He isn't," said Sally. "He stopped here while you were at Charlie Stewart's house. He just got the job of cutting Mr. Upjohn's lawn."

Mr. Upjohn always won several first prizes at the monthly Garden Club flower show. He grew his beautiful flowers in his large back yard, which he kept completely hidden by a high wall of bushes.

"I've been dying to see his flower beds,"

said Encyclopedia. "With Nevin working there, I can sneak a look."

"We'll sneak two looks," said Sally. "I'm going with you."

Mr. Upjohn was very rich. The detectives came upon his big house from the rear. Encyclopedia could see nothing but the roof above the bushes. Hearing Nevin's power mower, he got off his bike and parted the branches.

Nevin wasn't in the back yard. But Mr. Upjohn's daughter, Marybelle, a sixth-grader, was there with a hose. She aimed it and *swis-s-h-t-t*. A stream of water sprayed over Encyclopedia.

"Next time don't go poking your nose where it doesn't belong!" Marybelle said, laughing.

"Blug-a-luggle," gargled Encyclopedia. Red-faced and soaked, he climbed back on his bicycle.

"That Marybelle Upjohn!" said Sally. "She makes my fist itch!"

"Scratch it on her, and you'll get Nevin in trouble," said Encyclopedia as they rode to the front of the house.

Nevin saw his friends and stopped the lawn mower. "Were you attacked by a fire

"Were you attacked by a fire hydrant?"

hydrant?" he asked the dripping Encyclopedia.

"By Miss Smarty," said Sally, "What's she doing back there? She never worked in her life!"

"Her father asked her to water his flowers for two hours," replied Nevin. "He's paying her. She told me she is getting more money than I am when she hooked up the hose a few minutes ago."

The hose, Encyclopedia saw, was hooked to a water outlet by the garage. Like a long green snake, it ran across the driveway and disappeared into the bushes that walled off the back yard.

"Marybelle warned me to be careful of the hose," said Nevin. "She told me it was brand new and cost a lot of money."

"Marybelle always brags about how much things cost," said Sally, fuming. "She's probably sitting in a lawn chair eating jelly beans instead of watering the flowers."

"Maybe she's sleeping in a chaise lounge," said Encyclopedia. "It's none of our business what she's doing—"

"Hey, will one of you kids guide me into the garage?"

Encyclopedia saw a truck backing toward the Upjohn's garage.

"I'll help," he called to the driver.

With Encyclopedia giving signals, the truck inched backward and stopped.

"Don't stop there!" shouted Encyclopedia. "Your front wheels are on top of the new garden hose."

The driver, however, had hopped out of the truck. He glanced at the green hose. It was squashed flat under the front tires.

"The hose is rubber," said the driver. "It won't break. Besides, I'll be only a few minutes."

It took him five minutes to unload several large boxes, which he stacked against the wall of the garage. He was gone when Marybelle's mother drove up.

She parked her car in the garage and went into the house. A short time later she rushed out. Her mouth was open like a trunk.

"Nevin!" she called. "Come here at once!"

Nevin shut off the lawn mower. He ran to the front door and disappeared inside with Mrs. Upjohn.

When he came out, he looked close to tears.

"Mrs. Upjohn said I broke a valuable Chinese vase," said Nevin. "She said my father will have to pay for it."

"Why does she blame you?" asked Encyclopedia.

"She said she had the vase by the kitchen sink when she left the house fifteen minutes ago," answered Nevin. "She said I broke it getting a drink of water. But I didn't go into the house."

"Marybelle!" said Sally. "She did it, and she's afraid to own up!"

"Marybelle claims she didn't go into the house either," said Nevin. "She said she never stopped hosing the flowers in the back yard while her mother was gone."

"Marybelle is lying," said Encyclopedia.

"Can you prove that?" asked Sally eagerly. "You couldn't see her behind those bushes."

"I didn't have to see her," said Encyclopedia.

HOW DID ENCYCLOPEDIA KNOW?

(Turn to page 109 for the solution to The Case of the Chinese Vase.)

The Case of
the Blueberry Pies

Encyclopedia was shocked. He had just seen Chester Jenkins *running* past the detective agency.

Chester never ran—except to the school cafeteria at lunch hour. He was the biggest eater in the fifth grade.

He was also the roundest. In fact, Chester was nearly as high lying down as standing up.

Encyclopedia hurried out to the sidewalk. He looked up and down the block. There wasn't an ice cream truck in sight.

"What's wrong, Chester?" he called.

Chester stopped. He turned around and wobbled back. He was puffing like a marching band.

"I'm in training," he gasped. "I have to be in shape for the Idaville Youth Fair tomorrow."

"Charlie Stewart entered his tooth collection in the hobby contest," said Encyclopedia. "Are you in a running race?"

"Not exactly," replied Chester. "I'm getting in trim for the pie-eating contest."

Encyclopedia was puzzled. Why roadwork? Chester was a cinch to win. Only Belly Slave, the hippopotamus at the zoo, could eat more.

"Do you remember how sick the Thompson twins, Jimmy and Johnny, became last year?" asked Chester. "Their mother said the pie-eating contest was disgusting. She said there ought to be a physical fitness contest instead."

Encyclopedia remembered last year. Chester had left the other boys lying on their backs covered with pie crumbs. The Thompson twins had to be carried home.

"The rules have been changed," said Chester. "This year each boy has only two pies to eat. But he must run half a mile to the finish line."

"Hopping hamburgers!" exclaimed Encyclopedia. "That's a tough break, Chester."

"Those Thompson twins are fast runners," said Chester. "But if apple pie is used, I'll have a good chance. Apple pie is my favorite."

"Here's to apple pie!" said Encyclopedia.

"Thanks," said Chester, and grimly resumed his running.

The next morning Encyclopedia and Sally biked to the Idaville Youth Fair. It was a city of tents and fun rides crowded into one corner of the old airstrip.

The two detectives watched the kite-flying contest and the pet show. At ten o'clock a whistle blew for the pie-eating contest.

Fifteen boys lined up to hear Mrs. Thompson, the mother of the twins. She explained the new rules.

Each boy was to race to the table opposite him. On each table were two pies. The boys were to eat the pies, using the knives and forks provided, and then run a half-mile course among the tents.

"Most of the running will be out of view of the judges," said Mrs. Thompson. "But a father will be stationed every two hundred yards to make sure no boy takes a short cut."

The knives and forks troubled Encyclopedia. "Last year Chester won bare-handed," he said to Sally. "Table manners will slow him down."

"The silverware is Mrs. Thompson's idea," said Sally. "She said eating with the hands is a disgrace."

"Chester still has a chance if the pies are made with apples," said Encyclopedia. "Apple pie is his favorite."

"They're blueberry pies," said Sally. "Mrs. Thompson baked them herself. She said she didn't want anyone getting sick."

Encyclopedia saw Chester's chances fading as the boys crouched at the starting line.

"On your marks," said Mrs. Thompson. "Get set . . . go!"

Fifteen boys dashed for the tables.

Chester got off to a bad start. He was the last to reach the pies, and he fumbled his knife and fork.

After the first mouthful, however, he settled down. He began to eat smoothly, showing the form which had won him last year's contest. Knife and fork flashed like lightning. He overtook the other boys rapidly.

"He's ahead!" screamed Sally. "Go, Chester!"

"Say," said Encyclopedia, frowning. "I see only one of the Thompson twins."

Sally looked at the pie eaters carefully. "You're right," she said. "Which twin is missing, Jimmy or Johnny?"

"Don't ask me," said Encyclopedia. "I can't tell them apart. Come on, Chester!"

Chester was eating like a true champion. He was the first to finish both pies. He wiped his face and started on the half-mile course. In a moment he was lost behind the rows of tents.

The second boy to finish eating was the Thompson twin. He wiped his face, jumped from the table, and sprinted after Chester.

Three other boys finished their pies. But they could not run more than ten feet. The rest gave up at the table.

The race was between Chester and the twin!

"Go, Chester! Go!" screamed Sally.

"Chester has a minute headstart," whooped Sally. "There's nobody who can hold his pies like Chester!"

So it seemed as Chester eventually staggered into view again, still leading. Ahead of him stretched one hundred yards of open ground to the finish line.

He was halfway there when the onlookers roared. The twin had burst into view, running like the wind.

Chester was wobbling gamely, but slowing down with every step. The twin sped past him and won by fifteen yards. Encyclopedia and Sally were stunned.

When the twin had caught his breath, he walked back and forth, shaking hands. His lips were parted in a wide smile of victory.

"He sure has beautiful teeth," said Sally grudgingly. "Look at him strut. You'd think he was on television doing a toothpaste commercial."

Encyclopedia stared bitterly at the twin's white-toothed smile.

"He'll be smiling on the other side of his face soon," said the boy detective. "Chester is the rightful winner."

"Did the twin cheat?" said Sally.

"The *twins* cheated," said Encyclopedia.

WHAT MADE ENCYCLOPEDIA
SO SURE?

*(Turn to page 110 for the solution to
The Case of the Blueberry Pies.)*

The Case of
the Murder Man

Cicero Sturgess, the greatest child actor in Idaville, entered the Brown Detective Agency. He bowed low.

"Your Majesty," he said.

"Huh?" said Encyclopedia.

"Your Majesty—that's the opening line of my play," said Cicero. "Trouble is, I can't think of a second line."

"Well, you've made a wonderful start," said Encyclopedia encouragingly. "Have you got a title?"

"*Murder Man*," said Cicero. "It's for the Children's Interfaith Night at First Church on Saturday."

"A play about murder?" asked Encyclopedia, astonished. "Wouldn't a play about

Sleeping Beauty be better for church? Benny Breslin could do the snoring."

"I'm not joking," said Cicero. "Reverend O'Meara said I could put on a murder play if it wasn't too messy."

"Drownings are very clean," said Encyclopedia. "Fit concrete shoes on the victim and toss him overboard—"

"I'm allowed one shooting," interrupted Cicero. "But what good is even one? My mother won't let me touch a cap pistol. Imagine me, the star, pointing a pistol and having to shout, 'Bang! Bang!'"

"You could use a silencer on the gun," suggested Encyclopedia. "Nowadays, all the murderers use silencers."

"That's the answer!" said Cicero jubilantly.

Then his expression drooped.

"Carole and Marla Kenin are going to tap dance," he said. "Ted Holquist will do bird imitations. Percy Arbuthnot will recite *The Highwayman*. There will be other acts, but the play will be the main attraction."

"And you have only a title and an opening line," said Encyclopedia.

"Writing is hard work," moaned Cicero. "I need a little help."

Encyclopedia knew what was coming next.

"Write a murder mystery—with me as the star," pleaded Cicero. "I've got a great idea! Let the audience try to figure out how the detective solved the crime!"

"That's a corny idea," objected Encyclopedia.

Still, Encyclopedia wanted to do his share at the Children's Interfaith Night. So after dinner he wrote what Cicero wanted. The play had an intermission so that the audience could try to guess the solution. It had one shooting. And it starred Cicero.

Saturday evening Encyclopedia sat in the Fellowship Hall of First Church. He was nervous as any author on opening night.

After Ted Holquist finished his bird calls, Sally Kimball carried out a big sign. It read:

MURDER MAN
By Leroy Brown
Cicero Sturgess as Langley
Pinky Plummer as Frazer
Hank Jones as the Detective
Jim Dunn & Phil Cord as Policemen

The lights went out. The curtain parted.

The scene on stage showed the inside of two apartment rooms at night. Between them was a hall with a window and a door marked "Stairs."

In one apartment Frazer was reading a newspaper. Across the hall in the other apartment, Langley was putting on a pair of black gloves. He picked up a pistol and slipped noiselessly out the door. He tapped softly on Frazer's door.

"I hope I'm not disturbing you," said Langley as Frazer opened the door. "I thought we might play a game of chess. Are you alone?"

"I'm alone," said Frazer. "I'll get the chess set."

Langley stepped in and closed the door behind him. He pulled out the gun. The silencer muffled the noise of the shot.

Frazer doubled over and fell to the floor dead.

Langley moved swiftly. He took a key from Frazer's pocket. He unlocked Frazer's desk and scooped out a bundle of cash.

Then he coolly telephoned the police.

"Hello? My name is Langley," he said.

Langley pulled out the gun.

"I'm telephoning from the apartment of Mr. Frazer at six hundred Grand Street. Frazer's been shot!"

Hanging up, Langley slipped from Frazer's apartment. He threw the gun out the hall window and stepped into his own apartment.

Smiling, he removed his black gloves. The money he hid under his mattress.

When a detective and two policemen arrived, Langley was waiting for them in the hall by Frazer's open door.

"I'm Langley," he announced.

"Oh, yes. I spoke with you on the telephone," said the detective. "What happened?"

"It was too hot to sleep," began Langley. "So I decided to go out to a late movie. As I stepped into the hall, a man dashed out of Mr. Frazer's door. He knocked me down, tossed the gun out the window, and raced downstairs. I saw Mr. Frazer through the open door. Finding him dead, I called you immediately."

After examining the body of Frazer, the detective asked, "May I use your phone?"

"Go right ahead," said Langley.

The curtain fell. The lights in the Fellowship Hall went on.

The detective stepped from behind the curtain. He stopped at the edge of the stage and spoke to the audience.

"I had every inch of the dead man's room gone over for fingerprints," he said. "Everything was photographed, including the desk. The bullet that killed Mr. Frazer matched the gun found on the street below the hall window."

The detective looked around the audience.

"After studying all the reports, I arrested Langley for murder," he said. "Can anyone tell me what his mistake was?"

ONLY ONE GIRL KNEW. DO YOU?

*(Turn to page 111 for the solution to
The Case of the Murder Man.)*

The Case of
the Million Pesos

Encyclopedia solved mysteries at the dinner table. He solved mysteries in the garage. He solved mysteries at the scene of the crime.

There were no other places in Idaville, he thought, to solve mysteries.

He was wrong.

There was second base.

While sitting on second base, he solved a robbery that had taken place in a country a thousand miles away.

Encyclopedia got his start as an international detective during an evening baseball game. His grounder slipped through

Benny Breslin at shortstop. Encyclopedia wound up with a double.

Tim Gomez, the next batter, ended the inning by striking out. The game was immediately called on account of darkness. The score was 12 to 3.

Encyclopedia sat down on second base, discouraged. Benny Breslin flopped upon the grass beside him.

"We were going good," said Encyclopedia. "All we needed were nine runs to tie."

"I'm glad they stopped it," said Benny, a home-run hitter. "I've raced around the bases five times. My legs are falling off."

Sally walked over from first base. She looked troubled.

"What's bothering Tim Gomez?" she asked Encyclopedia. "He struck out six times in a row. Something is on his mind."

"Baseballs," said Benny. "He fielded every fly with the top of his head. He didn't catch one all game."

"Be quiet," whispered Encyclopedia, for Tim was passing near them.

"Sorry," Tim apologized. "I played like a cow on crutches."

"Forget it," said Encyclopedia.

"Aren't you feeling well?" asked Sally.

"I'm worried about my uncle, Duffy Gomez," said Tim. "He's in jail in Mexico City."

Duffy Gomez, Mexico's greatest baseball player, in jail! Encyclopedia, Sally, and Benny were stunned by the news.

"What did he do?" asked Benny.

"The police say he robbed a bank," answered Tim. "But I don't believe it!"

"What does your uncle say?" asked Encyclopedia.

"He says he's innocent," replied Tim. "The police threw him in jail just the same. He's being framed!"

"By whom?" asked Sally.

"By a man named Pedro Morales. He's hated my uncle for years," said Tim. "Pedro was in love with my Aunt Molly. She turned him down to marry Uncle Duffy."

"So Pedro accused your uncle of robbing a bank," said Sally. "What a low way to get back!"

"Doesn't your uncle have an alibi?" asked Encyclopedia. "Can't he prove he was somewhere else when the bank was robbed?"

"He says he's innocent," replied Tim.

"He was at a movie. Nobody saw him, though," said Tim. "Uncle Duffy wears a fake beard when he goes out in public. If he didn't disguise himself, baseball fans would mob him."

"Being at a movie is a pretty weak alibi," said Encyclopedia regretfully. "Your uncle will have a hard time making a judge and jury believe him."

"The real robber is bound to be caught," said Sally. "Don't you worry, Tim."

"There isn't much time left," said Tim. "Uncle Duffy goes on trial next week. Pedro will testify against him."

Sally glanced at Encyclopedia for help.

"Don't ask me," mumbled Encyclopedia.

"You *can't* say no," urged Sally. "Give it a try, Encyclopedia!"

"I can tell you everything about the case," said Tim eagerly. "I've read the newspaper stories my uncle sent from Mexico."

Encyclopedia considered the problem; namely, trying to solve a bank robbery in Mexico while sitting on second base in Idaville.

"You can't do Tim's uncle any harm," said Sally.

Encyclopedia couldn't argue with that. "You win," he said. "Tell me what you know, Tim."

"The National Bank of Mexico City was robbed last month by two masked men. They got away with a million pesos in one-peso bills," said Tim.

"That's about eighty thousand dollars," exclaimed Encyclopedia.

"Two weeks later," continued Tim, "Pedro Morales says he passed my uncle's house. It was late at night. There was a light in the living room. Pedro says he saw my uncle arguing with another man."

"Did Pedro overhear what was said?" asked Encyclopedia.

"Yes, the window was open," replied Tim. "Pedro claims my uncle said that he had counted the money again that afternoon. His share wasn't half the million pesos—it was a thousand pesos short."

"What happened next?" said Sally.

"According to Pedro," said Tim, "the other man got excited. He threw some money into my uncle's face and shouted,

'There's a thousand pesos. I never want to see your ugly face again!' "

"How did Pedro know they were talking about the stolen money?" asked Encyclopedia.

"Pedro says he didn't know—then," replied Tim. "Some of the one-peso bills the man threw at my uncle flew out the open window. Pedro picked them up. On a hunch, he brought them to the police. The numbers on the bills proved they were stolen from the bank."

"If Pedro had some of the stolen money," said Sally, "he must have had something to do with the robbery himself!"

"I agree," said Encyclopedia. "Pedro lied. His story just doesn't add up!"

WHAT WAS PEDRO'S LIE?

*(Turn to page 112 for the solution to
The Case of the Million Pesos.)*

Solution to *The Case of the Marble Shooter*

Bugs Meany said he had never seen the marble shooter "before in my life."

Yet when Duke Kelly and Spike Larsen asked who he was, Bugs said he was "Algernon Kehoe."

That was Bugs's slip!

For when Encyclopedia spoke with Bugs in the clubhouse, he called the marble shooter "Al Kehoe."

"Al" is short for many names. A few are Albert, Aldrich, Alfonzo, Alfred, Alister, Alton, and Alvin.

Bugs could not have known—unless he had met Algernon before—that "Al" was short for Algernon.

Solution to *The Case of Bugs Meany, Detective*

Bugs claimed that it was the strange action of the squirrel which led to his finding the violin.

The squirrel, said Bugs, "backed down slowly" from the tree.

That was Bugs's lie!

Squirrels *never* back down a tree.

They always come down a tree headfirst!

Told this fact, Bugs admitted stealing the violin.

Not only didn't Bugs get the expected reward of ten dollars, he had to return Mario's twenty cents.

And that night he closed his detective business for good.

Solution to *The Case of the Underwater Car*

Encyclopedia had seen "four worn-out tires" on Mr. Starr's car.

The car, however, was "brand new."

Mr. Starr had outsmarted himself!

He had removed the new tires in order to sell them. Then he had put old tires on the car and wrecked it. He had chosen a spot where the car could not be recovered from the ocean.

He thought no one would find out. But he had not counted on Encyclopedia.

Acting on Encyclopedia's information, Chief Brown had divers bring up the old tires.

When he saw them, Mr. Starr confessed.

Solution to *The Case of the Whistling Ghost*

Rocky made up "the other boy."

The other boy could not have run "out the back door and into the woods" with the stolen camera, as Rocky claimed.

Remember the spider web which Fabius wanted to photograph? It was spun "across the lower half" of the back door.

Had the other boy really run out the back door, he would have broken the web!

Solution to *The Case of the Explorer's Money*

The thief brought eight gifts—the penguins. These he stuffed with the money and placed in the museum.

He came back to the house on the day of the sale. He bought the penguins. He expected them to be shipped to him. But the police arrested him instead.

How had Encyclopedia known where the money was hidden?

The thief made one mistake.

In a room filled with objects from Sir Cameron Whitehead's trips to the Arctic, only the eight penguins didn't belong.

Penguins live near the Antarctic, or *South* Pole—which Sir Cameron Whitehead had never visited—not near the North Pole!

Solution to *The Case of the Coffee Smoker*

Harry said, "I waited in the truck till the rain stopped. Then I came straight into the kitchen."

That meant he had to go through the water on either the front or the back walk.

However, his shoes were dry, not wet. He lighted a match off the bottom of one, remember?

When Encyclopedia pointed this out, Harry admitted he had been home all day. He had noticed Roscoe smoking and decided to blackmail him.

Rather than have his father learn he'd been too lazy to inspect the fishing nets, Harry promised not to tell Roscoe's mother about Roscoe smoking coffee grounds in secret.

Solution to *The Case of the Chinese Vase*

Marybelle claimed she was in the back yard hosing down the flowers all the time that her mother was gone from the house.

The truck driver, however, had parked so that the hose "was squashed flat" under his tires.

That meant no water was getting through the hose to Marybelle.

But Marybelle did not come to the front of the house to see what was wrong. So Encyclopedia knew she was not using the hose then.

Mrs. Upjohn telephoned the delivery truck company. The driver told her he had parked on the hose, as Encyclopedia said.

Marybelle admitted she had gone into the house to rest. Under her mother's questioning, she confessed to having knocked over and broken the Chinese vase by accident.

Solution to *The Case of the Blueberry Pies*

Encyclopedia knew the Thompson twin who finished the race was not the one who had eaten the blueberry pies.

At the finish, the twin had "beautiful white teeth."

Impossible!

The blueberries in the pie would have stained his teeth blue.

When Encyclopedia reported this to their mother, the twins confessed. They had switched places as the first twin ran past the model-car tent.

Chester was declared the winner. He received the first prize—a pie a day for a month from the Purity Bake Shop.

Solution to *The Case of the Murder Man*

Although Langley telephoned from Frazer's apartment, his fingerprints were not on the telephone.

He did not remove his gloves till after returning to his own apartment!

In Langley's own words, "It was too hot to sleep." So he had no reason to wear gloves ...

... Except to avoid leaving fingerprints!

Solution to *The Case of the Million Pesos*

Pedro's mistake was in claiming that Tim's uncle said that he had "counted the money again that afternoon," and that "his share wasn't half the million pesos."

Remember, the stolen money was in the form of one million one-peso bills.

Tim's uncle could not have counted half a million bills, his share, in one afternoon.

It would have taken him five days—counting day and night!

ABOUT THE AUTHOR

Since the publication of the first *Encyclopedia Brown* book in 1963, DONALD J. SOBOL had written roughly one book a year. In 1967, at a Children's Book Fair, he explained, "I began writing children's mysteries because the mystery element was really very small in the so-called mysteries that were written for children and I felt that this was a shame." In 1976, the *Encyclopedia Brown* series was the recipient of a special 1976 Edgar Allan Poe Award, presented by the Mystery Writers of America in recognition of these books as the first mysteries that millions of children read. In addition to the *Encyclopedia Brown* series, Mr. Sobol has authored over twenty books for young readers. A native of New York, he now lives in Florida with his wife and children. He has been a free-lance writer for eighteen years.

Match Wits with America's
Sherlock Holmes in
Sneakers

ENCYCLOPEDIA BROWN

With a head full of facts and his
eyes and ears on the world of Idaville, meet Leroy (Encyclopedia)
Brown. Each Encyclopedia Brown
book contains 10 baffling cases to
challenge, stymie and amuse young
sleuths. Best of all, the reader can
try solving each case on his own
before looking up the solution in
the back of the book. "BRIGHT
AND ENTERTAINING...." *The
New York Times*
By Donald Sobol

15138	ENCYCLOPEDIA BROWN BOY DETECTIVE #1	$1.75
15140	ENCYCLOPEDIA BROWN/CASE OF THE SECRET PITCH #2	$1.75
15141	ENCYCLOPEDIA BROWN FINDS THE CLUES #3	$1.75
15136	ENCYCLOPEDIA BROWN GETS HIS MAN #4	$1.75
15104	ENCYCLOPEDIA BROWN KEEPS THE PEACE #6	$1.50
15131	ENCYCLOPEDIA BROWN SAVES THE DAY #7	$1.75
15093	ENCYCLOPEDIA BROWN TRACKS THEM DOWN #8 Donald J. Sobol	$1.50
15107	ENCYCLOPEDIA BROWN SHOWS THE WAY #9 Donald J. Sobol	$1.50
15300	ENCYCLOPEDIA BROWN'S FIRST BOOK OF PUZZLES & GAMES Jim Razzi	$1.50
15099	ENCYCLOPEDIA BROWN'S SECOND BOOK OF PUZZLES & GAMES Jim Razzi	$1.50
15135	ENCYCLOPEDIA BROWN & THE CASE OF THE MIDNIGHT VISITOR #13	$1.75

Buy them at your local bookstore or use this handy coupon for ordering:

Bantam Books, Inc., Dept. EB, 414 East Golf Road, Des Plaines, Ill. 60016

Please send me the books I have checked above. I am enclosing $_____ (please add $1.00
to cover postage and handling). Send check or money order—no cash or C.O.D.'s please.

Mr/Mrs/Ms _____

Address _____

City _____ State/Zip _____

EB—7/81

Please allow four to six weeks for delivery. This offer expires 1/82.

Bantam Skylark Paperbacks
The Kid-Pleasers

Especially designed for easy reading with large type, wide margins and captivating illustrations, Skylarks are "kid-pleasing" paperbacks featuring the authors, subjects and characters children love.

15097	CHARLIE AND THE CHOCOLATE FACTORY Roald Dahl	$2.75
15097	CHARLIE AND THE GREAT GLASS ELEVATOR Roald Dahl	$1.95
15113	JAMES AND THE GIANT PEACH Roald Dahl	$2.50
15100	ENCYCLOPEDIA BROWN BOY DETECTIVE Donald Sobol	$1.50
15026	ENCYCLOPEDIA BROWN CASE OF THE SECRET PITCH Donald Sobol	$1.25
15060	ABEL'S ISLAND William Steig	$1.95
15106	BIG RED Jim Kjelgaard	$2.25
15067	DRAGON, DRAGON AND OTHER TALES John Gardner	$1.75
15089	A DREAM FOR ADDIE Gail Rock	$1.95
15050	EMILY UPHAM'S REVENGE Avi	$1.50
15008	IRISH RED: SON OF BIG RED Jim Kjelgaard	$1.95
15086	JACOB TWO-TWO MEETS THE HOODED FANG Mordecai Richler	$1.95
15050	THE EYES OF THE AMARYLLIS Natalie Babbitt	$1.75
15065	TUCK EVERLASTING Natalie Babbitt	$1.95

Buy them at your local bookstore or use this handy coupon for ordering:

Bantam Books, Inc., Dept. EB, 414 East Golf Road, Des Plaines, Ill. 60016

Please send me the books I have checked above. I am enclosing $_____ (please add $1.25 to cover postage and handling). Send check or money order—no cash or C.O.D.'s please.

Mr/Mrs/Miss_____

Address _____

City _____ State/Zip _____

SK–3/81

Please allow four to six weeks for delivery. This offer expires 9/81

MS READ-a-thon-
a simple way
to start youngsters reading.

Boys and girls between 6 and 14 can join the MS READ-a-thon and help find a cure for Multiple Sclerosis by reading books. And they get two rewards—the enjoyment of reading, and the great feeling that comes from helping others.

Parents and educators: For complete information call your local MS chapter, or call toll-free (800) 243-6000. Or mail the coupon below.

Kids can help, too!

- - - - - - - - - - - - - - - - - -

Mail to:
National Multiple Sclerosis Society
205 East 42nd Street
New York, N.Y. 10017

I would like more information about the MS READ-a-thon and how it can work in my area.

MS
Mystery
Sleuth

Name _____
                          (please print)
Address _____

City _____ State _____ Zip _____

Organization _____

BA-5/81

A Public Service Message from Bantam Books.